Praise for my other books

'Will make you laugh out loud, cringe and snigger, all at the same time'
-LoveReading4Kids

'and cheeky'
—Booktictac, Guardian Online Review

Waterstones Children's Book Prize Shortlistee!

'I LAUGHED SO MUCH, I THOUGHT THAT I WAS GOING TO BURST!'
Finbar, aged 9

'The review of the eight year old boy in our house... "Can I keep it to give to a friend?" Best recommendation you can get' -Observer

'HUGELY ENJOYABLE, SURREAL CHAOS'
-Guardian

I am still not a Loser
WINNER of
The Roald Dahl
FUNNY PRIZE
2013

First published in Great Britain 2013
This edition published in 2016
by Jelly Pie, an imprint of Egmont UK Ltd
The Yellow Building, 1 Nicholas Road, London W11 4AN

Text and illustration copyright © Jim Smith 2013
The moral rights of the author-illustrator have been asserted.

Set ISBN 978 0 6035 7165 7
Book ISBN 978 1 4052 6033 6

barryloser.com
www.jellypiecentral.co.uk
www.egmont.co.uk

A CIP catalogue record for this title is available from the British Library
Printed in Great Britain by the CPI Group

60285/2

Egmont is passionate about helping to preserve the world's remaining ancient forests.
We only use paper from legal and sustainable forest sources.

This book is made from paper certified by the Forest Stewardship Council® (FSC®),
an organisation dedicated to promoting responsible management of forest resources.
For more information on the FSC, please visit www.fsc.org. To learn more about
Egmont's sustainable paper policy, please visit www.egmont.co.uk/ethical

so over being
I am a Loser

introducing
Snailypoos

Barry Loser
Noses drawn by Jim Smith

Get your OWN ruler

My mum's embarrassing enough just being my mum, but now she's won this stupid Feeko's Supermarkets competition it's even worse.

Like the other day, when I was skateboarding home with my best friend Bunky and we went past a Feeko's and there was a poster of my mum, winking and holding up a packet of sausages.

invisisausages

Bunky

'Coowee, Barry!' said Bunky, holding
a packet of invisible sausages and
scrunching his face up, trying to do
a wink.

I rolled my eyes and they landed on another poster of my mum, wiggling her bum in a pair of Feeko's jeans.

'Tshhhhhh!' farted a bus as it drove past with a poster of my mum on the side. She was sticking her tongue out and putting a Feeko's chocolate digestive on to it.

I didn't used to mind her winking, or the way she dances, or how she sticks her tongue out when she's eating, but now that she's on posters everywhere it's completely ruining my keelness.

I picked up a snail that was having a little drink of a puddle and went to throw it at the poster of my mum winking, then changed my mind because I'm not a snail murderer.

'There you go, Snailypoos!' I said, sticking him on to my mum's bum and patting him on the shell so his whole head disappeared inside it.

'See you tomozzoid,' I said when we got to Bunky's road.

I was just about to do my goodbye face that makes Bunky wee himself with laughter, when I spotted Nancy Verkenwerken standing outside Bunky's house.

goodbye
face

Nancy Verkenwerken is Bunky's loserish new next-door neighbour.

like a paperclip
but for hair

loseroid
and a half

She's got glasses like Mrs Trumpet Face down my street, plus she collects stamps, which everyone knows is the unkeelest thing you can do apart from winking.

'Get your OWN tomozzoid!' shouted Bunky, and I snortled with laughter because ever since I borrowed his ruler in Maths and he said, 'Get your OWN ruler!' we've been saying 'Get your OWN ...' and then the thing we're talking about after it.

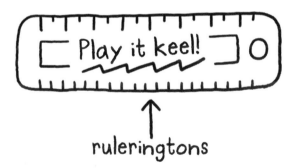

ruleringtons

I was still snortling as I rolled up to my front door and saw my mum through the kitchen window, holding a tin of chopped tomatoes like she was in one of her adverts.

about to be boiled to death

'Coowee, Barry!' she mouthed, doing a wink, and I stopped laughing and wished I wasn't the boy whose mum was The Voice of Feeko's.

Cupboard-eyes

'Do your helmet straps up!' shouted
my mum as I rolled off to meet
Bunky at the top of my road.

stinks

FEEKO'S Washing powder

Dad thought it was cereal

This was the next morning by the way, not that you could tell, because I was wearing all the same clothes, including my trousers that haven't been cleaned since my mum got her Feeko's job and my dad took over the washing.

'Do your OWN helmet straps up!' I shouted, all excited because it was less than a week until the school trip to The Ski Dome, which is the keelest place in the whole wide world amen.

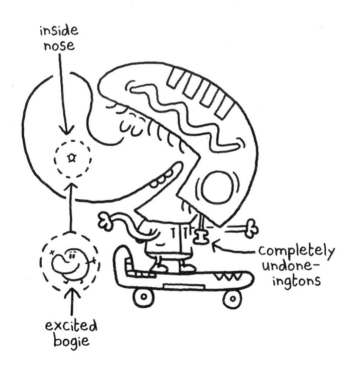

inside nose

completely undone-ingtons

excited bogie

The Ski Dome has its own hotel and indoor ski slopes with real-life snow, which was why Bunky was cycling towards me in a pair of ski goggles.

Bogies have glasses too

← Bunky

Nancy Verkenwerken was walking next to him with her Mrs Trumpet Face glasses on and a massive red stamp album under her arm.

'Ah, Mrs Trumpet Face, what do you have in your cupboard-eyes today?' I said to Nancy, and Bunky did a snortle.

'Cupboard-eyes' is what me and Bunky have started calling Mrs Trumpet Face's glasses, because the frames look like cupboard doors.

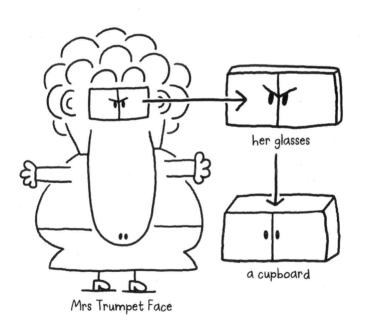

her glasses

a cupboard

Mrs Trumpet Face

'You, unfortunately,' said Nancy, pointing her cupboard-eyes right at me so I could see my reflection.

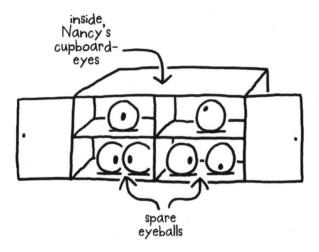

inside, Nancy's cupboard-eyes

spare eyeballs

Usually when I call Mrs Trumpet Face Cupboard-eyes she just stands there looking confused, so I didn't know what to do this time. I stood there looking confused until I felt something on my knee.

'OW!' I said, even though it didn't hurt. I looked down and saw a fly sitting on my trousers, eating a tomato ketchup stain. 'Arrrgghh, a fly!' I screamed, waggling my leg around like a sausage.

'It's more of a "sit" at the moment,' said Nancy, wafting her stamp album at it, and the sit turned into a fly and flew off.

'Thank,' I said, because it was only worth one thank, but Nancy was too busy looking at the old falling-apart house at the end of my road to take any notice. I glanced up at its windows and imagined a ghost staring down at me.

dead

'Come on Bunky, let's get the keelness out of here,' I said, pretending I wasn't scared, and we zoomed off, me with my helmet straps undone.

Cherry flavour puddle

One of the bad things about skateboarding to school is that you get there really fast, which isn't good when you're famous for having a famous mum.

'Here he comes, ladies and gentlemen!'
shouted Darren Darrenofski as me
and Bunky glided through the school
gates, and he ran up and poured
Cherry Fronkle on the floor in front
of me. 'A red carpet for our unspecial
guest!' he said, doing a wink and
wiggling his bum like my mum in her
adverts.

I flipped my board up and tiptoed through the Fronkle, wondering if Snailypoos would like a cherry flavour puddle.

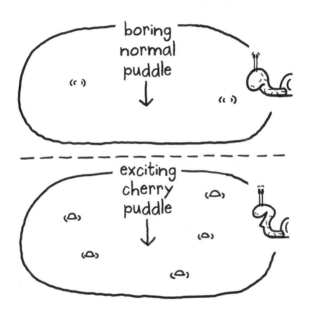

boring
normal
puddle

exciting
cherry
puddle

'What do you think of the new craze sweeping the school?' said Anton Mildew, holding a banana microphone up to my face.

Anton has been holding bananas up to people's faces and asking annoying questions ever since he started his newspaper, The Daily Poo.

'What craze?' said Bunky, sticking his nose in and waggling it about.

'The Mrs Loser Wiggle!' said Anton, and he danced around with his bum wiggling, sticking his tongue out and winking all at the same time.

bit of
ink on
paper

'Yeah, give us a wink, Loser!' said Gaspar Pink, who was standing behind Anton with his camera.

I watched them with my mouth shut and my eyes open and my bum completely still.

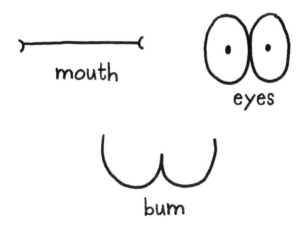

mouth

eyes

bum

'Nice helmet, Barold!' said Gordon Smugly, walking past and bonking me on the head so hard my legs did a wobble and one of my helmet straps flicked me in the eye and made me blink.

alien ⟶ •
planet

'Perfectamondo!' smiled Gaspar, and his camera flashed in my face.

Daily Poo snowball

Anton and Gaspar were fiddling around on the computer in the corner of the classroom when I walked in with Bunky, playing it keel times a million.

Gaspar

'Arrr! Good morning me hearties!' shouted Miss Spivak, who's been our teacher since Mr Hodgepodge went on a six-month cruise around the North Pole with my granny.

swoosh

same noses

There was a parrot on her shoulder and she was carrying a sword and had an eyepatch on and one of her legs was a wooden stump.

'What's good about it?' said the parrot, which was the only bit of Miss Spivak's outfit that wasn't weird, because he's our class parrot that we adopted from Mogden Zoo when it closed down last year.

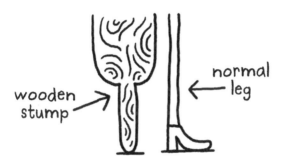

wooden stump

normal leg

'Well for starters it's Show and Tell,' said Miss Spivak, putting the sword down and pulling her leg out of the wooden stump. 'I'll go first. Can anyone tell me what this is? Yes, that's right, it's an eyepatch. Who knows why pirates used to wear them?' she said, all in one go.

'Me!' shouted Darren.

'Yes, Darren?' said Miss Spivak.

'I dunno,' said Darren, and we all did a little snortle.

'Was it for when they got a sword poked in their eyeball?' said Tracy Pilchard, jangling with jewellery like she was a pirate herself.

JINGLE

JANGLE

'That's right, Tracy. Mind-boggling, isn't it!' said Miss Spivak, poking the plastic sword into her eyepatch. It was one of those swords where the blade pushes into the handle, and everyone gasped.

'Mind-boggling!' screeched the parrot, whose name is Honk, and I thanked keelness the zoo closed down, otherwise we'd just have a hamster.

keelest
pet ever

most boring
pet ever

I'd forgotten it was Show and Tell, so I was rummaging around in my rucksack for something keel to talk about when I saw Anton's and Gaspar's stupid feet walking to the front of the classroom.

inside my rucksack

tiny apple

Dad's pen

tuna sandwich

Cherry Fronkle

ruleringtons

sharpener I found

Mum's pencil

squishy Not Bird

Thumb Sweet

this book

'Hot off the press!' said Anton,
holding up a sheet of paper with
'The Daily Poo' typed out at the top.

Underneath was a photo of me. My
bum was wiggling from where my legs
had gone wobbly, and I was winking
from the helmet strap that'd hit me
in the eye.

'Just like his mumsy!' said Gordon from the back of the classroom, and everyone laughed, and I rolled my eyes to myself because I know for a fact he calls his mum 'Mama'.

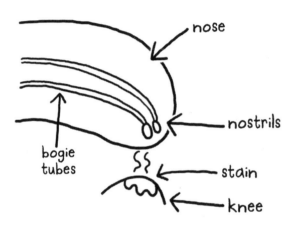

I was still rummaging around in my rucksack, which meant my nose was near my knee, and a waft of tomato ketchup went up my nostrils and gave me an amazekeel idea for how to stop them laughing.

There's a bit in every **Future Ratboy** episode where he treads in a dog poo and waggles his foot in the air.

'By the power of smelly shoe . . .' he shouts, and his enemies run off screaming.

'Get your OWN mumsy!' I shouted,
hopping up to the front of the
classroom with my leg bobbing around
in front of me.

my
knee

'By the power of smelly knee . . .' I said,
waving it in front of Anton's and
Gaspar's noses.

'Get a photo, Gaspar, he's gone
completely stark raving bonkers!'
said Anton, holding his Daily Poo up
to protect himself from my knee.

I grabbed the newspaper and scrunched
it into a snowball and aimed it at
Gordon Smugly's nose. The only
problem is, I'm rubbish at throwing.

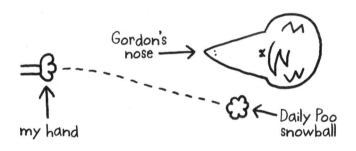

'Mind-boggling!' screeched Honk as the
snowball whizzed past his beak and hit
Miss Spivak in the eye, which luckily
for me was still underneath her pirate
eyepatch.

I glanced over at Bunky and high fived him with my eyes, which is what we do when something like this happens.

eye
hands

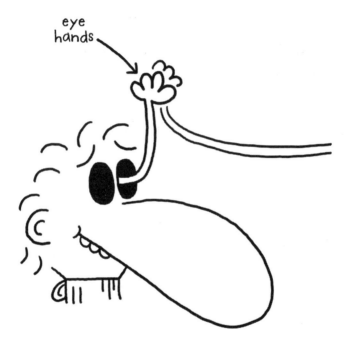

'That's it Loser, outside NOW!' screeched Miss Spivak, although it could have been Honk, because I wasn't really looking.

Barry Tiptoes

On my way to the door I walked past
Nancy Verkenwerken, who was going
up to the front to show off her
massive red stamp album.

I looked at my reflection in her cupboard-eyes and she smiled one of those smiles where you're not sure if the person is being nice or thinking what a loser you are.

nice

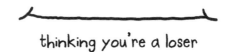

thinking you're a loser

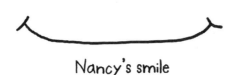

Nancy's smile

'Looking forward to The Ski Dome, Loser?' said Mr Koops, jogging past me as I stepped into the hallway, smelly knee first. His trainers squeaked on the floor like he was treading on parrots.

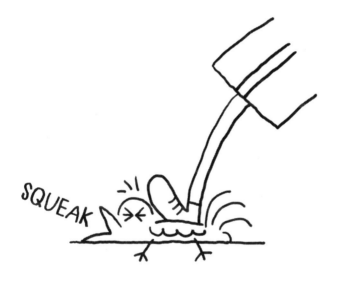

SQUEAK

'Ye-ah!' I said, splitting my yeah into two bits because of how excited I was.

'If you're anything like your mum you'll be a natural!' he shouted over his shoulder, and he tucked his arms in as if he was skiing and wiggled his bum like my mum.

Mr Koops's new moustache

I got on my tiptoes and peered through the little window at the top of the classroom door. Nancy was pointing to a stamp with a picture of a butterfly on it.

'Bor-ring,' I whispered, and the glass misted up from my breath.

Last year's Ski Dome photos were stapled up on the wall behind me, so I walked over to look at them, still tiptoeing because there was nothing else to do, plus I wish I was a bit taller, like Bunky.

me

Everyone in the photos was having the keelest time ever, and I imagined myself zooming down a ski slope in my new jacket and goggles, having snowball fights with real-life snow instead of scrunched-up Daily Poos.

I was snortling to myself about a photo of a snowman that looked exactly like Mr Hodgepodge, when the classroom door swung open and everyone ran out, all fizzy like Fronkle pouring out of a can.

staple city

'I'm gonna collect sweets!' said Stuart Shmendrix, wobbling past opening a packet of Cola Flavour Not Birds.

'I'm gonna collect jewellery!' said Tracy Pilchard, jangling from all her jewellery.

Thumb
Sweet

Flower
ring

Fronkle
ringpull

'I'm gonna collect Fronkle ringpulls!' said Darren Darrenofski, who drinks about five million cans of Fronkle a day, so that wouldn't be very hard for him.

1. flip hand upside-down

2. twizzle...

3. then reverse

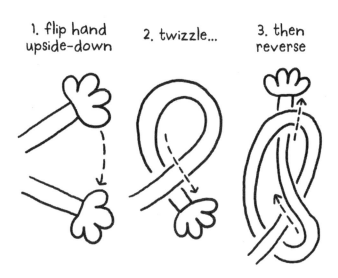

I was just about to do a reverse-twizzle-upside-down-salute from how loserishly excited everyone was about their stupid collections, when Miss Spivak came out with Nancy Verkenwerken.

'Well that went down well didn't it! Mind-boggling how many stamps you've collected. I think you might've started a new craze!' she said all in one go, patting Nancy on the head.

'Yeah, a craze for being a loser,' I said, doing a mini-salute in my pocket for how funny I was.

I looked at Nancy's eyes through the glass in her glasses and waited for her to say something clever or do one of her sort-of smiles.

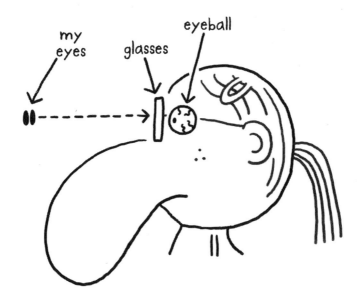

'Mind-boggling,' she whispered to herself, and she walked off towards the playground.

'Can I go now please?' I said, looking at Miss Spivak.

'I don't think so, Loser,' said Miss Spivak, then Honk the parrot said it too.

Brian's Burgers napkin

It was rubbish having to stay in the classroom with Miss Spivak for the whole of break, looking through the window at everyone in the playground coming up with their stupid collections.

'Blah-de-wee-wee-poo-poo-blah,' said Miss Spivak. I'd stopped listening to her telling me off and started watching Bunky instead, who was standing behind the glass doing his face that makes me wee my pants with laughter.

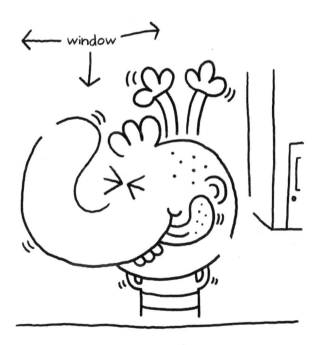

'BOR-RING,' he mouthed, and the glass in front of him steamed up and his fingertip drew a picture of Miss Spivak with a speech bubble saying 'Get your OWN ruler!'

still the window

The bell went and Bunky ran in all excited. 'I'm gonna collect tea towels!' he said, and I felt sorry for him for deciding to collect such a rubbish thing.

yawnsville

His drawing of Miss Spivak saying 'Get your OWN ruler!' was still on the window behind him, and it gave me one of my unbelievakeel ideas.

'I'm gonna collect rulers!' I said,
because if everyone was going to
have a collection, there was no way
I wasn't too.

'Too late, Loser!' said Sharonella, bonking me on the nose with her ruler, and I did a quadruple-reverse-twizzle-salute using all my hands and feet, because who wants to collect rulers anyway.

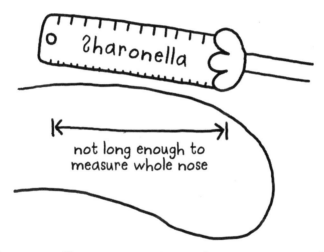

'I know, I'll collect **Future Ratboy** stuff!' I said, doing a little blowoff with excitement. 'I've got millions of **Future Ratboy** things, plus I'm his number-one fan!'

'NOT!' screeched a familiar voice from behind me, and I turned round to see Gordon Smugly holding up his plastic talking Not Bird.

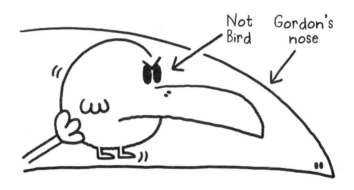

Not Bird

Gordon's nose

'Think again, loseroid!' said Gordon, then I realised it was his plastic talking **Future Ratboy** that he was holding up in his OTHER hand.

I spent the whole rest of the day like that, coming up with something keel to collect then finding out someone already collected it, so by the end of school I was desperadoid.

I was skateboarding home and had just done a jump over a dog poo and was wondering if I could get away with collecting dog poos, when I spotted something out of the corner of my eye.

Two paving stones across from the poo was a napkin, lying there like a snail had put it down to have a picnic. I bent over, holding my breath so I didn't smell my tomato ketchup knee, and picked it up, careful not to scrunch it into a snowball.

The napkin said 'Brian's Burgers' on it, and there was a picture of Brian doing a massive smile from eight million years ago before he went completely bald.

Brian on
napkin

Brian
now

I thought of all the other places
that have their own napkins with keel
stuff on them, and how I've always
liked napkins because you can tuck
them into your collar like a mini **Future
Ratboy** cape, and I did my smile I do
to myself when I've just worked out
what I'm going to collect*.

*Can't be bothered to draw smile.

Detective Inspector My Mum

I tucked the napkin into my collar and zoomed home, doing turbo-fear-blowoffs as I went past the old falling-apart house.

My dad was tying his tie up in the mirror when I got in, which was weird because he's usually taking his tie OFF at that time of day.

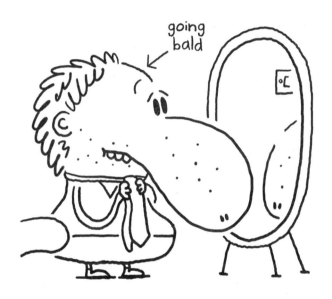

going bald

'How keel is this napkin!' I said, and he scrunched his face up like I was a complete Loser, which I am, thanks to him.

Suddenly I sensed something mum-like to my right, and I turned round and saw my mum coming down the stairs in her new pink dress and high heels.

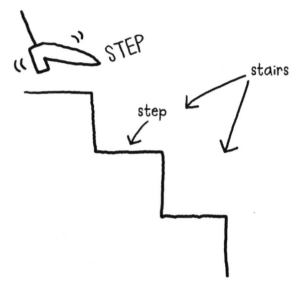

I'd been so busy trying to work out what to collect, I'd completely forgotten we were going to Toppolino's restaurant for my mum and dad's three-millionth wedding anniversary.

'How keel is my Brian's Burgers napkin!'
I said, holding it up, and she peered
down at me, looking all disappointed
with her son, who is me.

Great
Aunt
Loser

'Have you been skateboarding with
these undone?' she said, feeling my
helmet straps to see if they were
warm, like the detective in her
favourite TV show.

'No-o!' I said, splitting my no into two bits, because I was lying.

I whipped my helmet off and threw it on to the coatrack, also like the detective in my mum's favourite TV show.

Starring
Mike Lamppost

'I got a call from Miss Spivak today...'
said my mum, her voice like a parrot
being strangled, and I scrunched my
face up, not like the detective in her
favourite TV show at all.

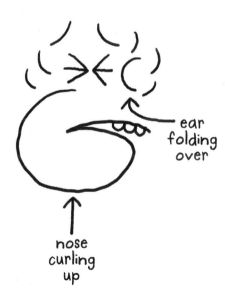

ear
folding
over

nose
curling
up

Toppolino's restaurant

'Mr and Mrs Lootzah!' said Flavio as we walked into Toppolino's, and the whole restaurant went quiet, everybody glancing over at my mum and doing the Feeko's wink to each other. 'I see you the big TV actress now!' he whispered, and she did her nervous laugh and went the same colour as her dress.

keel!

TOPPOLINO'S

crazy
paving

'Bay-ry! Still playing it keewel?' said
Flavio, pinching my cheek.

'OW!' I shouted, and I was just about
to do another ow and split it into two
bits because of how much it hurt when
I spotted a Toppolino's napkin on the
table next to me and did a blowoff
out of excitement.

'What are we going to drink?' said my dad, sitting down and looking at the menu with his worried face because he hates spending too much money, and I came up with an amazekeels idea to make my mum completely forget about how naughty I'd been at school.

same fly that landed on my knee

Menu

'Waiter! Champagne for everyone and a can of Fronkle for me!' I shouted, clicking my fingers in the air like **Future Ratboy** when he's in a restaurant.

Flavio

CLICK!

'BARRY,' whisper-shouted my mum, and she smiled at everybody in the restaurant but did her scary eyes at me. 'Just a bottle of the house wine,' she said to Flavio, and I saw her hand scrunch a napkin into a half-snowball.

Pizza with meatballs on top

I always order the same thing when we go to Toppolino's, which is why I was eating a pizza with meatballs on top when I saw a bus going past outside.

The advert on it was my mum's Feeko's one where she's sticking her tongue out and putting a chocolate digestive on it.

I rolled my eyes to myself, remembering the photo of me on the front of Anton's Daily Poo, and brought a slice of pizza up to my mouth.

me doing what I was just saying

All of a sudden one of the meatballs started rolling off the slice, like a giant snowball falling down a mountain.

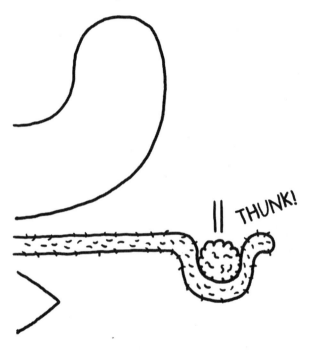

THUNK!

The meatballs are my favourite bit of Toppolino's pizza with meatballs on top, so I stuck my tongue out to catch it.

'Just like his mama!' said Flavio,
wobbling past carrying a dish with
flames coming out of it, and I heard
the man on the table next to us do a
snortle.

I looked down at my magic smelly knee
and got ready to turn him into a snail.

TA DA!

'BARRY!' whisper-shouted my mum again, glaring at me like she knew what I was thinking.

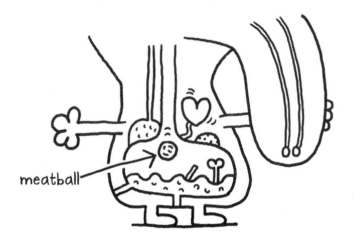

meatball

I swallowed my meatball and did a burp, but not on purp, which is short for purpose by the way.

'So Barry, The Ski Dome's next week!'
said my dad, changing the subject.
'How kewel is that!'

'It's KEEL, not KEWEL,' I said, because
I was still in a bit of a mood from
my mum glaring at me, and my dad
scrunched his face up like he felt like a
Loser, which he should do, because he is.

my dad's
business card

A. LOSER

Flavio wobbled up with our puddings
all balanced on one arm.

Mine was coconut ice cream, which
I don't even like, but I'd got it anyway
because it looked like snowballs.

can't be bothered
to draw hair

'Mmm, delish!' said my mum, sticking her tongue out and putting a spoonful of Knickerbocker Glory on to it.

I heard the man on the table next to us do another one of his snortles, and even though I knew it probably wasn't about my mum, it made my knee wake up.

'Yours looks nice,' said my mum, digging her spoon into one of my snowballs.

Ever since I was minus nought, I've always hated it when someone helps themselves to my coconut ice cream, and I felt my magic smelly knee start to waggle.

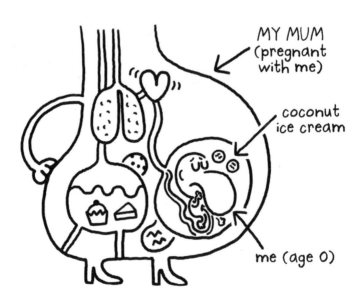

MY MUM (pregnant with me)

coconut ice cream

me (age 0)

My mum scooped out a mini-snowball and hovered it towards her mouth, which was opening so that her tongue could stick out and make the man laugh again.

'Get your OWN pudding!' I shouted, and the whole of Toppolino's went quiet apart from the noise of my mum's glaring.

Some-thing happens

My mum was completely and utterly silent in the car on the way home from Toppolino's, and the same at breakfast the next morning too.

She didn't even shout 'Do your helmet straps up!' as I rolled off on my skateboard with a Toppolino's napkin in my collar, so I didn't do them up, not that I ever do anyway.

playing it keel times 8 million

It was a relief to get to school
after all that silence, and I even
pretended not to get annoyed when
Darren Darrenofski came in with a
poster of my mum from Feeko's that
he'd cut into a mask and strapped on
to his ugly face.

my
mum

me

Darren

'Coowee, Barry!' he shouted, and
everyone sniggled but didn't do the
Mrs Loser Wiggle because of how busy
they were with their new collections.

Not Bird
pencil
topper

Toppolino's

Brian's
Burgers

I'd just laid my Brian's Burgers and Toppolino's napkins out on my desk, ready for people to ask about if they were interested, when Mr Koops jogged into the classroom in his squeaky trainers.

'Hands up who's going to The Ski Dome on Monday!' he shouted, and I put my hand up and waggled it around.

I spotted Nancy Verkenwerken's hand sitting on her desk doing nothing at all, and thanked keelness it wasn't mine.

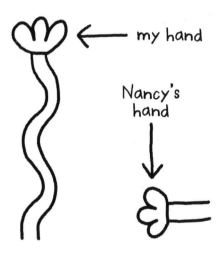

'Coach leaves nine sharp!' said Mr Koops, and he jogged out again.

After that I spent the whole day talking about skiing and napkins, and a little bit about tea towels to keep Bunky happy.

really bored

Then it was home time, so I put my helmet on and skateboarded out of the school gates with the Bunkmeister, blowing off with keelnosity.

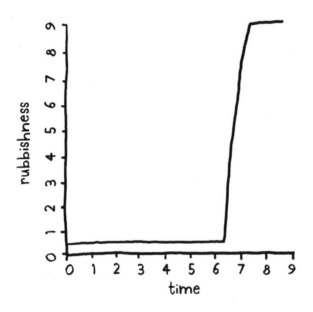

You know when everything's going along all nicely then something really bad happens?

Standing on the pavement like a
Feeko's cardboard cut-out of herself
was my mum, talking to Miss Spivak.

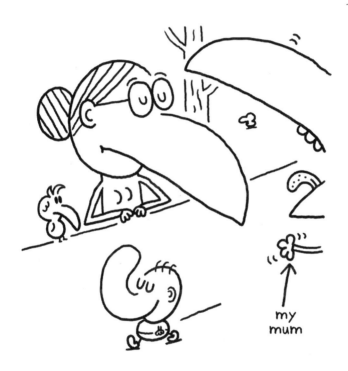

my
mum

I started doing my helmet straps up
before she could see they were undone,
but it was too late.

The next thing I knew, I was in the back of the car and my mum was zooming us out of town.

'Where are we going?' I screamed, worried she was driving me to the dump like our old fridge that time.

contents: Feeko's lollies

HUMMMMM

THUMP

I tried to open the door and do a
Future Ratboy roll out of the car, but
the locks were on, so I started banging
on the sunroof with my helmet, which
was still on my head by the way.

'We are going shopping,' she said, smiling to herself, and I looked out of the window and saw a sign to Mogden Mall.

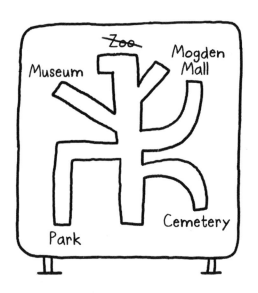

Unkeelness to the max

Whenever I'm really naughty, my mum takes me to Mogden Mall.

It's where all the mums go to do their clothes shopping, and it's the most boring place in the whole wide world amen.

'Do your helmet straps up,' said my mum once we'd parked and got out of the car.

'There's no skateboarding allowed,' I said, pointing to a sign that said 'No Skateboarding Allowed in Mogden Mall', and I did my face I do when there's a sign that says what I've just said.

'Do your helmet straps up,' said my mum again, like she was her own parrot, and she smiled her smile she smiles when she's about to make me look like the biggest loser ever*.

* Still can't be bothered to draw smile.

It's bad enough walking around
Mogden Mall with a mum who's
famous for sticking her tongue out
and wiggling her bum in the Feeko's
adverts, but walking around it with a
done-up helmet on and no skateboard
is unkeelness to the maxingtons.

I was waggling my magic smelly knee around, trying to turn myself into a snail, when I sensed something mum-like to my left, which was weird because my mum was on my right.

I glanced over and saw a Feeko's window with a massive poster of my mum sticking her tongue out and putting a prawn cocktail crisp on it.

POINT

'Hey, that's you!' said a man walking past who looked like Father Christmas but in normal clothes. 'Hey everyone, it's the Feeko's lady!' he shouted, pointing at my mum and then the poster, and I thought how this was my worst day ever, because now Father Christmas was ruining my life too.

I stood there as a crowd started gathering round my mum and I pretended I was a cardboard cut-out Barry, because I don't think cardboard can get embarrassed.

'Do the bum-wiggle dance!' said someone from the crowd, and I saw my mum shake her head and go pink, and I thanked keelness that at least THAT wasn't going to happen.

'Bum-wiggle! Bum-wiggle! Bum-wiggle!'
shouted the crowd, and I saw faces
leaning over from the other floors to
see what was happening.

I looked at my mum, and she did her
smile she does when she's about to
make me look like the biggest loser
ever times ten.

'OK, I'll do it!' she said, and the whole of
Mogden Mall went silent.

Disasteroid at Mogden Mallingtons

'Noooooooooooo!' I screamed, ripping the helmet off my head and throwing it on the floor. The trouble is, I'm rubbish at throwing.

'Look at it go!' shouted someone from the crowd as it flew towards a businessman holding a cup of coffee.

'Arrggghhh, my cappuccino!' he screamed as the helmet knocked the cup out of his hand, raining coffee on to an old lady walking out of a coat shop.

'My new fur coat!' she shrieked, opening an umbrella, which shocked a pigeon that was pecking at a chip on the floor.

The pigeon squawked and flew into a fake Christmas tree, even though Christmas wasn't for ages. The tree wobbled like Flavio the waiter, and one of its baubles dropped.

WHOOSH

'My baby!' roared a man with a pram, because the bauble was heading straight for it.

'I'll save your baby!' boomed Father-Christmas-with-normal-clothes-on, pushing through the crowd and diving across the pram, catching the bauble in his hood.

LEAP!

'Hooray!' shouted someone from the crowd, even though Father-Christmas-with-normal-clothes-on had landed in a wheelie bin and was hurtling towards the poster of my mum sticking her tongue out and putting a prawn cocktail crisp on it.

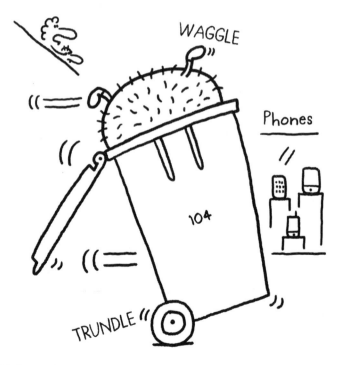

A noise like a man crashing into an enormous Feeko's window echoed around Mogden Mall as I pulled my hood over my head like a snail disappearing into his shell, and my mum did her smile she does when she isn't smiling at all.

Everything being all muffled

I kept my head inside my hood for the whole weekend after that, which meant everything I heard was muffled.

Like when Father-Christmas-with-normal-clothes-on stumbled out of the hole in the window and mumbled, 'I think I'm OK,' it was muffled.

And when my mum shouted that I was in big trouble in the car on the way back from Mogden Mall, that was muffled too.

ZOOM

When we got home and I was sent to bed and my mum and dad stayed up downstairs talking about what to do with me, it was even more muffled than usual.

And when I woke up the next day with my mum and dad telling me I WASN'T GOING TO THE SKI DOME because I'd:

1. Thrown a Daily Poo snowball at Miss Spivak

2. Ruined their anniversary meal at Toppolino's

3. Not done my helmet straps up

   AND

4. Made Father-Christmas-with-normal-clothes-on smash into a Feeko's window at Mogden Mall

it was muffled like in a bad dream, and my vision was all blurry, but not because I was crying or anything.

Barry Hood

'If you're not going then neither am I,'
said Bunky when I told him on the way
to school on Monday.

'Don't worry about me, you go and have fun!' I said, completely lying.

Not that it mattered once we'd got through the school gates, because Bunky zoomed off and was in the coach and ready to leave before I could do a triple-reverse-upside-down-back-to-front-salute inside my pocket.

fully inside shell

The coach did a smoke blowoff as it crawled out of the school gates, and Bunky waved from the back window, doing his face that usually makes me wee myself with laughter. But I just stood there like a cardboard cut-out of me, because cardboard can't cry about not going to The Ski Dome.

'Don't leave meeee . . .' wailed Sharonella, dropping to her knees on the pavement as Tracy and Donnatella blew kisses through the window.

thinks she's in a film

Tears rolled down her cheeks and on to the pavement, and I wondered if Snailypoos would like a cry flavour puddle.

'Have a napkin,' I said, passing her a spare one I'd picked up at Mogden Mall before the helmet-throwing disasteroid.

'Thanks, Barry,' she said, and she blew her nose like a grandad.

A Feeko's carrier bag was flying around in the sky, and I wished it was me, because then I could float off and land next to The Ski Dome, wherever that was.

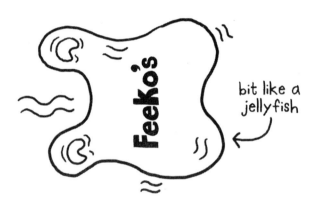

bit like a jellyfish

The bag swooped past Nancy Verkenwerken, who was waving goodbye to Bunky and Anton Mildew.

'Look after my Daily Poo!' mouthed
Anton, and Nancy pointed to a badge
on her jumper that said CHIEF OF POO
in big capitals.

Underneath in little letters it said
'Temporary Editor, The Daily Poo'.

I looked at her with her massive red stamp album and had one of my genius ideas.

CHIEF OF POO

Temporary Editor,
The Daily Poo

'I s'pose you have spares of those,' I said, walking over and pointing at her stamps. She turned her cupboard-eyes towards me and I saw myself in their reflection.

'I suppose I might,' she said, starting to turn round and walk off.

'Maybe I could pop round your house after school and have a little chat about them,' I said, feeling all keel like the detective in my mum's favourite TV show, and the Feeko's bag swooped down from the sky and shlopped me in the face.

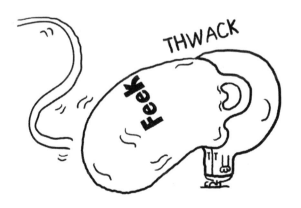

Worst plan ever

It was weird walking down Bunky's road after school knowing he wasn't there.

I looked up at the sky and saw a plane fly past and imagined him inside, even though they'd gone by coach.

I knocked on Nancy's door then realised she wouldn't be in, because I'd skateboarded from school and she was walking.

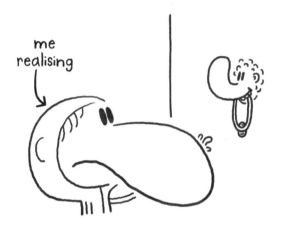

me realising

'Hello?' said a voice from inside.

'It's Barry Loser,' I said, and I heard the voice do a sniggle, probably because of how loserish my stupid name is.

'I'm meeting Nancy to talk about a top-secret plan,' I said, and the door opened.

'You'd better come in then, hadn't you,' said Nancy Verkenwerken except twice the height and more mum-like.

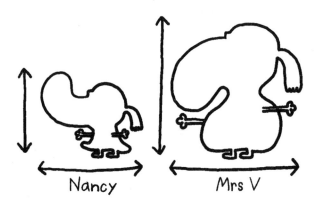

Nancy   Mrs V

Nancy's house was exactly the same as Bunky's but flipped round the other way and filled with different stuff, including a baby. 'This is Keith,' said Mrs Verkenwerken.

'Nice to meet you, Keith Verkenwerken,'
I said, and I did a little sniggle myself,
because of how loserish HIS name was.

The front door slammed and Nancy
walked into the room.

'Oh HE'S here,' she said, kissing
Mrs Verkenwerken on the cheek and
sticking her tongue out at Keith.
She turned round and ran upstairs, so I
followed her because I'd completely had
enough of sitting on my own with
Mrs Verkenwerken and Keith.

'What do you want, Barry?' said Nancy, flumping down on her bed. There was a map of the world above her desk with eight million pins stuck in it.

that map I was just talking about

'Are they the places you want to visit?' I said, and she rolled her eyes inside their cupboards.

'No, they're the countries where people don't ask stupid questions,' she said, making herself smile, and I smiled too, because that's the sort of keeloid thing I'd say to Bunky.

'OK, here's the plan,' I said, sitting down at the desk. 'I borrow some of your spare stamps and stick them on my forehead, then I write the address of The Ski Dome on my nose and climb into a postbox. As long as I try and look all envelopey I'll be there by tomozzoid!'

Saying it out loud made me realise that maybe it wasn't the keelest plan ever.

Barry
Envelope

'That is the worst plan I have ever heard in my entire life,' said Nancy, throwing a pillow at my head. 'I thought Bunky was stupid!' she laughed, and I felt my knee start to waggle.

'So what's YOUR plan, Cupboard-eyes?' I shouted, then I went quiet, because I wanted to know what her plan was.

Posting myself skiing

I don't know why Nancy thought my plan was so unkeel, because hers was exactoid the same except a billimetre better.

'Take a deep breath!' she giggled, squishing me into the cardboard box she'd got from her loft. We'd cut a hole in the front for my massive nose to stick out, and two in the bottom for my legs.

In the corner Nancy had stuck millions of her spare stamps, and underneath she'd scribbled, 'the ski dome'.
On the top in big capitals it said, 'CONTENTS: LOSER'.

'I can't see!' I snortled, wobbling down the street towards the postbox.

'Watch out for the dog poo,' said Nancy, and I thought how Bunky would probably make me walk straight into it. 'The postman comes in ten minutes,' she said as I lowered myself down next to the postbox.

I twitched my nose twice, which meant 'OK', even though I could've just said the word out loud. 'Good luck!' she whispered, and I heard her little feet walk off.

Then I was alone.

You know when you're sitting in a pitch-black cardboard box all by yourself in the middle of the street and it's completely boring? That's what was happening to me when I heard something snuffling.

Caffeine Free Diet Vanilla Fronkle

POST

A dog had his nose right up against the box, next to the bit where my smelly knee was.

'By the power of smelly knee . . .'
I whispered, waggling it as much as
possible, but I don't think he turned
into a snail.

really
enjoying
himself

WOOF

'Woof!' barked the dog, and I curled
myself into a ball and imagined I was
on the ski trip.

WHOOSH!

← having best
time of
whole life

I was just about to stick my legs
through the holes and run off
screaming like the world's most loserish
box, when there was a jangle of keys.

'Shoo, pooch!' shouted a familiar voice,
and I wondered if the dog had
suddenly learned to speak, but I don't
think he had because he whimpered
and I heard his four little feet run off.

'Hmm, this is most unusual,' said the voice, and I felt it kick the box.

I stayed as still as possible and hoped my sticking-out nose didn't look too nose-like.

CONTENTS:
LOSER

totally
looks like
a nose

the
ski dome

'"CONTENTS: LOSER",' the voice read out, chuckling, and I rolled my eyes to myself, because that was the second time someone had laughed at my stupid name that afternoon.

I'd just finished rolling my eyes, which can make you feel a bit dizzy, especially if you do it inside a pitch-black cardboard box, when everything started to wobble.

'Unngggh,' heaved the voice, and I felt myself floating through the air. 'That's one hea-vy Loser,' it said, plonking me into the back of a van.

I knew it was a van because I'd been in a van before, when my dad hired one to take our fridge to the dump, and it smelled exactly the same as this.

My nose has got a good memory like that, which isn't always a good thing, especially with dog poos.

My tummy rumbled as the engine started, and I thought how it was probably dinner time at home, but I didn't care because I was going skiing.

Snowball Barry

I was surprised when the van stopped and the engine turned off and the voice said, 'Here we are!' because I was expecting the drive to The Ski Dome to be much longer than two minutes.

'Oooooff,' breathed the voice as I starting floating again, and I did a little snortle, patting myself on my smelly knee.

I couldn't wait to see Bunky's face when I jumped out of the box in the middle of the ski slope and rolled down to the bottom like a snowball Barry.

that snowball Barry thing I was just talking about

A doorbell rang, and I tried to remember if The Snow Dome would have a doorbell and decided it must have.

'Hello,' said the man who answered the door, who sounded just like my dad.

'I found this package,' said the first voice, and I suddenly realised the reason it was familiar was because it belonged to my postman, Deirdre, who isn't a postman at all, she's a postwoman. 'I think it might be yours?'

Barry Parrot

I ate my dinner from inside the box after that, ignoring my mum and dad every time they talked to me.

I could tell they were feeling guilty for not letting me go skiing, because they kept saying things they thought might cheer me up.

'I was thinking we could go to Gnome Kingdom after school tomorrow,' said my dad, and I twitched my nose three times, which means 'Gnome Kingdom is for loseroids'.

'Ooh I almost forgot, I got you this,' he said. I punched a fork into my box and looked through the four little holes at a napkin with 'Cooky's Cookies' written on it. My dad gets a cookie from Cooky's every lunchtime, which is why he's so fat.

'Kewel or what!' he said, holding his knife like Miss Spivak's sword, and I thought of Honk sitting on her shoulder, which gave me one of my brillikeel ideas.

'KEWEL OR WHAT!' I said, like a parrot in a cardboard cage.

Lesser
Spotted
Barry

'That's what I just said,' said my dad, all excited because I was speaking.

'THAT'S WHAT I JUST SAIDYPOOS!' I Honk-squawked, saying what my dad had just said, but adding some poo.

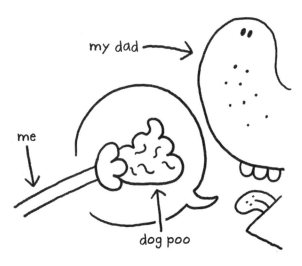

'Oh, I get it,' said my dad.

'OH. I GET YOUR OWN GET IT!' I said, and I saw his knee start to waggle.

'Stop that Barry,' said my mum, making a noise like she was drying a plate with a tea towel, and I wondered if Bunky would want it for his loserish collection.

'DON'T STOP THAT BARRY!' I said, not stopping it at all.

'Oh for . . .' said my dad.

'OH FOR FIVE, SIX, SEVEN, EIGHT, NINE, TEN!' I said, even though I can count to thirteen million and seventeen.

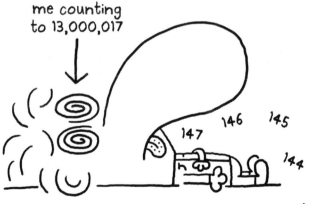

me counting to 13,000,017

147 146 145 144

'Barry!' shouted my mum, and I shouted, 'BARRY!' and then, 'IS THE KEELEST!' and I ran upstairs to bed inside my box, because if I wasn't going to The Ski Dome, I might as well go to sleep for the rest of my life.

Non-Bunky losers

My mum didn't have to shout 'Do your helmet straps up!' as I rolled away on my skateboard the next morning, because I'd already done them up.

'Have a good day!' she shouted instead, and I shouted 'HAVE A RUBBISH DAY!' back, saluting myself for being so funny.

The trouble with skateboarding to school with no Bunky is that you get there even faster than ever, so I was glad when I glided past Feeko's and spotted a reason to be late.

'Snailypoos!' I shouted, floating over
to the poster of my mum wearing a
pair of Feeko's jeans. The snail I'd stuck
on her bum had been there the whole
time, squiggling slime all over the glass.

just
woken
up

'You can be my new best friend,'
I whispered, picking him up by his
shell and squelching him on to my
skateboard, and I zoomed off,
Snailypoos's eyes waggling in the wind.

'I thought you'd be in The Ski Dome by now,' said Nancy as I walked into the classroom. Everyone was doing drawings apart from Honk, who was sitting on Miss Spivak's shoulder making the noise of a pencil.

'I THOUGHT YOU'D BE IN THE SKI DOME BY NOW!' I Honk-squawked as I laid my napkins out on my desk and popped Snailypoos into my pencil case, and Nancy scrunched her face up, all confused.

← Snailypoos

Play it keel!

I looked at all the non-Bunky losers sitting around me and rolled my eyes to myself.

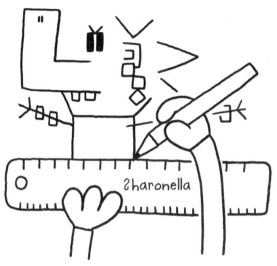

Sharonella was drawing Tracy Pilchard and Donnatella, but with all straight lines because of her stupid ruler collection. They were waving from the top of a ski slope, and I imagined Tracy's jewellery-noise echoing around the dome.

Next to me, Stuart Shmendrix was sucking on one of the sweets from his sweet collection, which is more of a sweet WRAPPER collection if you ask me, which you didn't.

BANG   BANG

He was jiggling his knee, banging it against the desk leg so the whole thing wobbled.

'Get your OWN knee,' I mumbled under my breath, waggling my magic smelly one, and Nancy snortled.

I grabbed my skin-coloured colouring pencil and was about to start drawing Bunky when I realised the lead bit was blunt, so I reached into my pencil case and pulled out the sharpener, doing a mum-glare at Stuart's annoying knee the whole time.

You know how a snail shell is the same size as a pencil sharpener and has a pencil-sized hole in it like a sharpener does too?

snail

sharpener

'Snail murderer!' gasped Gaspar Pink, his camera doing a flash.

I looked down at my hands and saw Snailypoos with the skin-coloured pencil up against his face like a miniature Miss Spivak's sword.

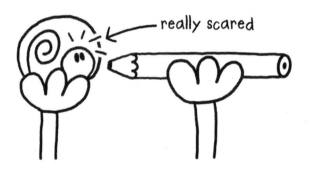

really scared

'Snailypoos!' I screamed, dropping the pencil and stroking his shell, and he wagged his slimy tail.

'This is going in The Daily Poo!' shouted Gaspar, looking around for Anton then remembering he was skiing, and I was just about to bonk him on the head when Nancy Verkenwerken stood up.

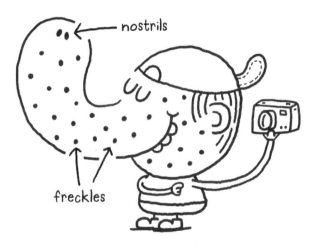

nostrils

freckles

'I don't think so Gaspar,' she said, pointing at her CHIEF OF POO badge, and I thought how maybe she wasn't such a complete and utter loseroid after all.

Cardboard cut-out Barry

I spent the rest of the day pretending Snailypoos was Bunky, which was boring with a capital yawn, so I was glad when I spotted Nancy at the end of my road after school.

She was staring up at the scary
house, scribbling something in a little
notebook. I skateboarded up and stood
behind her, playing it keel to the max.

'It must be hard being a Loser,'
she said, not even looking at me.

'**ME** A LOSER? YOU'RE THE ONE WHO WEARS MRS TRUMPET FACE GLASSES AND COLLECTS STAMPS!' I shouted, wishing I hadn't stopped to say hello, not that I'd even said hello yet. She giggled and carried on scribbling.

doesn't like it when I shout

'WHAT ARE YOU LAUGHING AT?' I screamed, waving my arms around like Tracy in Sharonella's drawing.

'You've got a snail on your head,' she said, and I patted my helmet and felt Snailypoos's shell with my hand.

I turned two of my fingers into snail-eyes and followed a slime trail all the way from Snailypoos's bum, over my helmet, along the strap, across my shoulder and down my jumper into my pocket, which was where I'd last put him.

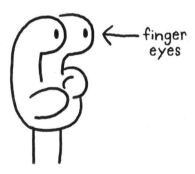

finger eyes

'And I meant that it must be hard having Loser as a second name,' she smiled.

'Oh,' I said, feeling a bit stupid, which is something Nancy is good at making me do. 'Yeah, well . . .' I mumbled, because it IS hard being a Loser, not that I am one. 'My grandad used to say that HIS grandad got the name because he was always losing things,' I said, and I sniggled, because my grandad was funny like that.

Great Great
Grandad Loser

'Mind-boggling!' said Nancy, scribbling it down in her book. 'That'd make a nice story for The Daily Poo,' she said, pushing her glasses on to her forehead, and I saw Snailypoos in their reflection, sitting on my head.

happier now

The windows in the scary house were behind Nancy, staring down at me like enormous cupboard-eyes. 'Are you doing a story on the scary house?' I said, blowing off in secret.

'Sort of,' she said, and I felt myself turn into a cardboard cut-out, because cardboard can't get scared.

Smeldovia

It was the next lunchtime and I was sitting with Nancy and Snailypoos under the big tree in the playground, eating a packet of crisps and picking my nose.

I'd collected all my bogies together into one massive fly-sized one and stuck two crisp crumbs into it for wings. 'Look, it's that fly that was eating the tomato ketchup off my knee!' I said, buzzing it around in front of her nostrils.

'You really are a revolting little Loser, aren't you,' said Nancy, wafting at it with her big red stamp album. The fly-bogie flew out of my hand and landed on a leaf.

crisp crumb

bogoids

'Why are you so interested in the scary house?' I said, the words coming out of my mouth without me even saying they could.

'I thought you'd never ask!' she said, twisting round to face me. 'You remember my map, the one with all the pins?'

I nodded, even though I couldn't see what that had to do with anything, plus I was already getting a bit bored.

'They're all the places I've collected stamps from,' she said, opening her album and pointing at a space on the last page. 'I've got every country except one.'

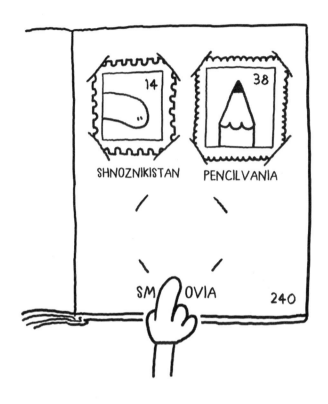

Under the space in her best capitals was the word 'SMELDOVIA'.

'It's a tiny island in the middle of the ocean,' she said.

'Smeldovia? That's the unkeelest
name in the whole wide world amen!'
I laughed, doing a snort-laugh by
accident. Then I stopped, because I
could see she was serious, plus I felt like
a bit of a snortoid from my laugh.

fridge
eyes

'I heard my mum talking to Deirdre the
postman about the scary house, and
guess what . . . The old lady who lives
there is SMELDOVIAN!' said Nancy, her
cupboard-eyes lighting up like fridges.

A shiver went down my spine, or maybe it was Snailypoos going for one of his walks. 'Oooh, excuse me while I wee myself,' I said, pretending I wasn't scared.

not going for a walk ⟶

'She gets a letter from her sister in Smeldovia once a week. All we have to do is sneak up to her bin in the middle of the night and get the stamp off the envelope!' she said, and I suddenly wished I hadn't made friends with Nancy Verkenwerken to begin with, thank you very much indeed times ten.

Even worser plan ever

You know how it was lunchtime before? Well now it was teatime, not that you could tell because I was still wearing all the same clothes, including Snailypoos on my head.

Nancy and Gaspar were sitting at my kitchen table, with me opposite wishing I could melge the two of them together to make a robot Bunky.

PLAY. IT. KEEL.

'Does he HAVE to be here?' I whisper-shouted to Nancy, Snailypoos's eyes pointing at Gaspar. I could see the reflection of my face in Nancy's glasses, and I looked scared.

'This is gonna make a great story for The Daily Poo. We'll need photos!' she whispered back.

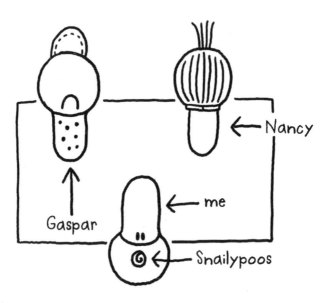

'Barry's favourite!' said my mum, winking and bringing over three bowls of coconut ice cream.

hair →
looks like
ice cream
↓

'BARRY'S NON-FAVOURITE!'
I Honk-squawked, and my mum scrunched her face up like a napkin. It was getting dark, and I saw Nancy's cupboard-eyes glancing out of the window.

Gaspar took a photo of his ice cream and I remembered me being on the front of The Daily Poo, which was the beginning of how I'd got myself into this mess in the first place.

'So what's the plan for this evening?' asked my mum, wiggling her bum to the song on the radio.

'Oh not much,' said Nancy, not splitting her oh into two bits, even though she was lying, because the plan was this:

1. Climb out of my bedroom window after dinner

2. Tiptoe up to the scary house

3. Rummage around in the bins

4. Find an envelope with a Smeldovian stamp on it

5. Get the keelness out of there without being eaten by a ghost

'BOR-RING!' said my mum, and I Honk-squawked it, my voice all wobbling.

The scary house

'I could be on the sofa playing it
keel watching **Future Ratboy**,'
I whisper-shouted, limping up to the
gate of the scary house.

I'd bonked my knee jumping out of the
bedroom window and landing in my
dad's compost bin.

'Shhh,' shushed Nancy, creaking the gate open and tiptoeing down the path to the front door, gravel scrunching under her feet.

how to
draw
a shhh

'Shhh,' I mouthed to Nancy's feet and I did a salute to myself for being so funny.

'This is where she puts her envelopes,' whispered Nancy, pointing at a green plastic container piled up with paper.

Gaspar carefully lifted his camera and pointed it at the box. There was a tiny click then everything went white. The whole garden had lit up from the flash.

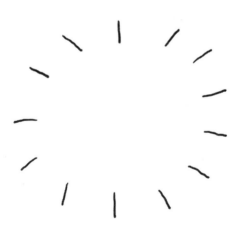

I looked at Nancy's cupboard-eyes, reflecting the camera flash like two TVs, then glanced behind her. An enormous black hole had appeared on the side of the house.

'It's going to eat us!' I tried to scream, but nothing came out, then I stopped trying to scream, because I'd realised that the black hole was just Nancy's shadow.

I limped over to the container,
feeling a bit loserish, and lifted up a
flattened-out cereal box. I spotted a
soggy old napkin underneath. 'Keelness
times a million!' I mouthed, and I was
about to do a double-reverse-under-
arm-salute when a spider the size of
Snailypoos ran up my arm.

'Arrrgggghhhhh!' I whispered, waggling
my elbow and hopping around on my
good leg. My hood flopped down and I
saw Snailypoos roll on to the grass like
a christmas tree bauble.

'Don't tread on Snailypoos!' mouthed Nancy, searching through a pile of old bills and looking a bit scared herself. I froze into a cardboard cut-out of a ballerina on one foot, and Gaspar took another photo.

Snailypoos

'There's a good boy,' I whispered, picking up Snailypoos all shakily and dusting his shell off. His little head was all the way inside, but I could tell he was OK.

Nancy stopped rummaging and twizzled round, doing a jiggle like she needed a wee, except she was doing it because she was happy. In her hand was an envelope with the Smeldovian stamp on it.

boringest stamp ever

The Old Lady
Scary House
Mogden

'Let's skedaddle,' whispered Gaspar, snapping a photo of the stamp and backing off down the path, looking like he wanted his mum.

Suddenly a light came on in the upstairs window and I saw a shadow against the wallpaper. It was moving, very slowly, across the room. A shiver went down my spine, but I knew it wasn't Snailypoos going for one of his walks, because he was still in my hand.

'That's the old lady's bedroom,' mouthed Nancy, grabbing my wrist and heading towards the gate.

You know how sometimes when you're really scared, all you want to do is run away, but for some reason your legs won't move? That's what was happening now.

A massive shiver went down my arm, whipping Snailypoos out of my hand and into the sky.

'Snailypoos!' I whisper-screamed, watching in slow motion as he floated past my nose like a scared little moon.

WHOOSH

A light came on in the hallway behind the front door and I heard a jangle of keys.

'I'LL SAVE YOU, SNAILYPOOS!' screamed Nancy, and I jumped and did a blowoff from how loud she was.
She was leaping into the air and diving towards him with her envelope open like Father-Christmas-with-normal-clothes-on's hood.

For a millisecond there was silence, then the sound of a snail landing inside an envelope.

'Phew,' I said, wiping my hand across my forehead like **Future Ratboy** when he's just got out of trouble. Then there was the sound of a front door creaking open.

'Let's get the keelness out of here!' giggled Gaspar, scrunching down the path, and we raced after him, limping and blowing off with fear, although that might've just been me.

How does it hang-eth?

The scary house didn't look as scary the next morning when I met Nancy at the end of my road. She held her big red stamp album up and patted it, smiling.

'Still wish you'd stayed in and watched **Future Ratboy**?' she said as we got to the school gates, and I was just about to split my NO into two bits when a coach did a smoke blowoff and crawled into the car park.

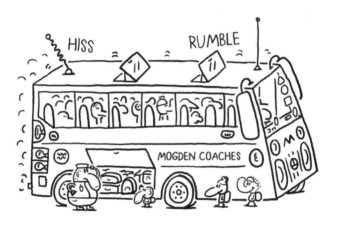

The doors hissed and everyone that hadn't been at school all week poured out, fizzier than the fizziest can of Fronkle ever.

'How's it going, Barold?' said Gordon Smugly, walking past and bonking me on my helmet, just missing Snailypoos.

'What a loser,' whispered Nancy in my ear, but I was too busy watching Bunky, who was standing with Anton and Darren, doing a loserish poking thing with one of his fingers.

'Get your OWN ruler!' I said, walking over with my limp. I was making it look worse so I had something to talk about.

'Barry! How does it hang-eth!' said Bunky, talking all weirdly.

I put my hand up for him to high five. 'Keelness as usualoid!' I said, and Anton sniggered.

'We say SKIEL now,' said Bunky, poking fingers with Darren. 'It's like playing it keel, but skieler-eth.'

POKE

'Skiel,' I said, putting my finger up for him to poke, but they'd turned around and started getting their bags out of the coach by then, so I folded my finger up and put it back in its pocket with all the other ones.

The Skiel Gang

'I am SO tired from the coach-eth,'
said Anton at lunch, and Nancy rolled
her eyes at me, because everything
they'd said since coming back was
either about skiing or had an 'eth'
on the end.

'Me too-eth,' said Darren, guzzling a can of Fronkle. I don't think he'd had one all week, because this was about his fiftieth already.

He ripped the ringpull off the can and clipped it on to the inside of his jacket, which is where he keeps his loserish collection.

secret lining

Bunky was scraping his mashed potatoes into a ski slope and dotting peas on it to look like skiers.

'Yeah, I'm really tired too-eth,' I said, trying to join in, plus I wanted to tell them about the scary house from last night.

'You don't-eth even know what tired is until you've done a day's skiing,' said Bunky, flicking a pea, and it landed in a splodge of brown sauce on the table.

'BOR-RING,' mumbled Nancy under her breath, and I smiled at her, but only because I'm so nice.

Darren balanced the pea on to his finger like a bogie and held it up for Anton to poke, but Bunky nodded to where I was sitting and Darren's finger twizzled round to face me.

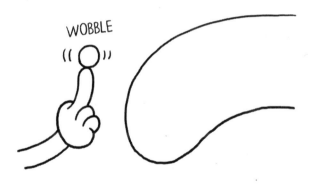

'Sounds like somebody called Nancy Verkenwerken is jealous they didn't go skiing,' he smiled, waggling the pea in front of my nose.

I looked at Bunky, who was doing his face that makes me wee my pants, then at Nancy, who was staring at me like my mum, all disappointed in her son, who isn't me.

'Yeah Nancy, play it skielingtons!' I said, poking Darren's pea-bogie.

The pea popped and green slime oozed
out, snailing down my finger and
landing on my trousers, not that that
mattered seeing as they stank already.

Nancy picked up her stamp album and
rolled her cupboard-eyes to herself.
'Mind-boggling,' she whispered, walking
away on her little feet.

Unskielness to the max

Everyone was reading The Daily Poo the next day as I rolled into school with Bunky, playing it skiel-eth times a million.

I was just about to pick one up when I heard something annoying and ugly behind me.

'Happy birthday-eth to-eth me-eth,'
sang Darren, pouring himself a Cherry
Fronkle carpet as he marched through
the gates. 'Party at my house Saturday
night-eth,' he burped, handing out
napkin-sized bits of paper.

birthday
bogie

Bunky grabbed one and I got on my
tiptoes to have a look.

In the middle was a photo of Darren in
The Ski Dome, next to a snowman that
looked exactly like Miss Spivak.

'Skielness to the max!' I said, because it
was an invite to a skiing fancy dress
party, which meant I had a reason to
wear my completely unused ski clothes
after all, thank you very much indeed
amen.

'Practising your ballet, Barold?' said Gordon Smugly, waggling a copy of The Daily Poo in my face. I focused my eyes on to it and saw a photo of me in front of the scary house, balancing on one leg like a cardboard cut-out ballerina.

everyone reading it

In capitals at the top were the words 'BARRY LOSER: SCARED OF HIS OWN SHADOW!' and underneath it said 'Story by Nancy Verkenwerken'.

'Get your OWN-eth Barry-unskielness!' snortled Bunky, poking fingers with Darren, and I felt my knee start to waggle. I rolled my eyes around, looking for Nancy, and spotted her through the classroom window, sitting at a desk with her stupid stamp album.

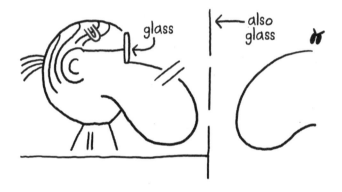

She pointed her cupboard-eyes at me, and even though there were two sheets of glass between us, I could tell that she could tell that I could tell she could tell what I was thinking.

Get your OWN snail

'I thought we were friends!' I shouted, marching into the classroom, holding up The Daily Poo.

'So did I,' said Nancy, licking her finger and turning a page in her album. I saw the Smeldovian stamp and snortled, but not one of my nice snortles.

me keeping it keel

'You wouldn't even have that if it wasn't for me,' I said, putting my hand into my pocket to give Snailypoos a pat, because he doesn't like it when I'm angry.

Nancy getting all angry

'Oh please, all you did was stand there panicking. No wonder you're a Loser!' she laughed, and it all went quiet. 'Sorry, I didn't mean that,' she mumbled, but I wasn't really listening, because Snailypoos wasn't in my pocket.

I dropped to my knees and started scrabbling around under the desks. 'Snailypoos!' I screamed, spotting a pencil sharpener, and I put it in my pocket, because you can never have too many of those.

'Where did you last see him?' said Nancy, her feet standing next to me looking worried, and I scrunched my face up like a napkin.

'Get your OWN snail,' I shouted, pulling my hood over my head, and I ran out of the classroom, everything waggling.

The slime trail

A slime trail from where I'd been standing with Bunky zigzagged out of the school gates and down the pavement. I was just about to run after it when I heard the sound of trainers squeaking behind me.

'School's this way, Loser!' said
Miss Spivak. Honk was on her shoulder,
doing the noise of Mr Koops's shoes.

She twizzled me round, and I limped
back to the classroom, my eyes all
blurry.

slime trail

Everything was muffled for the whole rest of the day until the bell went at home time and I zoomed out of the gates like a skier racing down a mountain.

no Snailypoos

Bunky was cycling behind me, telling me one of his boring Ski Dome stories. I hadn't told him about Snailypoos because I didn't want him to think I was a loser, and I sort of wished Nancy was there instead, because at least she'd understand, even though we weren't friends any more.

'What in the name of playing it unskiel are we doing-eth?' he said as we skidded up to Mogden Cemetery.

The slime trail zigzagged through the gates and on to the grass, then disappeared amongst the gravestones.

MOGDEN
CEMETERY

There were millions of them, lined up like Fronkles on a shelf, and I knew there was no way I was going any further without my mum and dad holding both my hands, and maybe my feet too.

A shiver went down my spine, and I patted my back, but Snailypoos wasn't there.

It was starting to rain, and a drop landed on my cheek. 'Let's get the unkeelness out of here,' I said, remembering how much Snailypoos liked puddles, so at least he'd be OK until tomorrow.

me and Bunky
(behind rain)

'See you at Darren's party tomozz-eth!' said Bunky at the top of his road, doing his face that usually makes me wee my pants with laughter.

'Get your own tomozz-eth,' I said,
and I rolled off, not snortling.

from
Granny
Harumpadunk

I could see my mum through the
kitchen window when I got home,
reading a postcard with an iceberg on
the front, and I wondered if Nancy
would've liked the stamp on the back.

'What's wrong with my little Snookyflumps?' she warbled, stretching her arms out, and I thanked keelness she wasn't a cardboard cut-out, because cardboard can't tell when you need a hug.

Have you seen this snail?

I spent the whole of Saturday with my mum and dad, holding their hands in Mogden Cemetery and putting up Lost Snail signs, calling out Snailypoos's name.

My voice was wobbly and my vision was blurred, but I didn't care times a million.

photo by
Gaspar

I wasn't even embarrassed when we were sticking a poster to a lamp post outside Feeko's and three teenagers with squidged-pea spots recognised my mum from her adverts.

'Do us your wink!' said the one with braces, and my dad hid behind the lamp post, probably because we were sticking up Lost Snail posters, which is about as unkeel as you can get, apart from collecting stamps.

FEEKO'S Superdupermarket

really greasy

'We'll find him, Snookyflumps,' said my mum as we drove home, but I just stared at a raindrop zigzagging down the window like an invisible Snailypoos.

PITTER PATTER

I trudged upstairs and put my ski clothes on all slowly. 'It won't be the same without you,' I said, looking at myself in the mirror.

still no Snailypoos

My helmet was on with the straps done up, but Snailypoos wasn't sitting on top any more.

Just like Mumsy

My mum's car did a smoke blowoff as it drove up to Darren's flats and I got out. 'Have fun!' she mouthed through the window, doing a wink, and I winked back, keeping one eye open for Snailypoos.

That's what I was doing, standing there winking, dressed in ski clothes, looking for Snailypoos in the pitch black with a shiver going down my spine, when I heard a familiar voice from behind me.

'It must be hard being a Loser,' said Nancy, and I turned round and saw a pair of cupboard-eyes in the middle of a bright-red ski outfit.

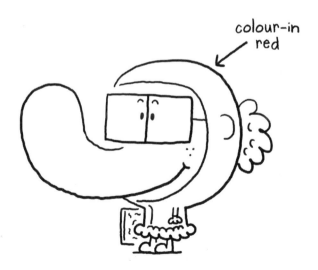

colour-in
red

She opened her album and took out a stamp with the keelest picture of a snail on it ever. I limped over to take a closer look.

'I thought you could call him Snailypoos Two,' she said.

that stamp I was just talking about

I pulled my ski glove off and pinched the stamp between my fingers, all carefully like I would with Snailypoos.

'Thank times a million,' I said, looking through the glass in Nancy's glasses, into her little cupboards.

A bus did a fart in the distance, reminding me of my mum sticking her tongue out in her chocolate digestive advert.

'Just like Mumsy,' I said as I opened my mouth and poked my tongue out, licking the stamp and sticking it on to my helmet, keelness-style.

Darren's party

'Welcome to the Darrenofski residence!'
said Darren except twice the height and
more dad-like, opening the door with
his elbows because he was carrying
so many Fronkles. 'Have a Fronkle!'
he smiled, passing me and Nancy a
can each.

BOOM
BOOM
BOOM
BOOM

I'd never been round Darren's before, so I didn't know his flat was on the seven-trillionth floor. We trudged up the stairs behind Mr Darrenofski, panting because of all our ski clothes.

'Bazzoid and the Nancemeister!'
shouted Bunky as we walked in.
'This is the skielest party ever-eth!'

I limped over to the window and looked at the view. You could see the whole of Mogden from Darren's living room, including a Feeko's Supermarket, and I snortled to myself because a poster of my mum was winking at me, holding up a packet of sausages.

Smeldovian airlines

I was just about to split my snortle into two, because I was thinking how Snailypoos was out there somewhere having a nice cup of puddle, when I sensed something Bunky-and-Nancy-ish behind me.

'Fancy-eth a boogie?' said Bunky, walking over with Nancy and putting his arms round our shoulders.

I jumped, because I was still a bit nervy from when the spider had run up my arm about four days ago, and the Fronkle flew out of my hand into the air.

I stuck my other hand out, trying to catch it, but punched Nancy in the nose by accident instead.

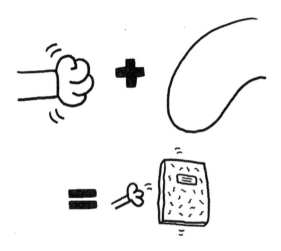

'My stamp album!' she screamed, dropping it as Fronkle poured down like cherry rain.

And that was when I remembered Father-Christmas-in-normal-clothes.

'I'll save it!' I shouted, diving towards the album.

I gave myself a salute in my head as I flew through the air and caught the album in my hood, landing helmet-first in a bowl of prawn cocktail crisps.

biggest bowl ever →

CRUNCH!

'By the power of playing it keel!' I yelled, standing up and waving the album in the air. I looked around to see how impressed everyone was and spotted something land on my non-smelly ski-outfit knee.

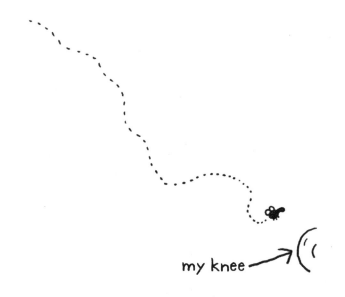

my knee

'Arrrggghhh, a fly!' I screamed, waggling my leg like a party sausage, and that was when I noticed a big red rectangular thing slipping out of my hand.

Fronkle splash

'Noooooo!' screamed Nancy, running towards me in slow motion. I turned my head and saw the album falling, also in slow motion, into a massive bowl of Fronkle punch.

A splash the size of Darren Darrenofski's dad jumping into a bath exploded out of the bowl and all over Gaspar Pink.

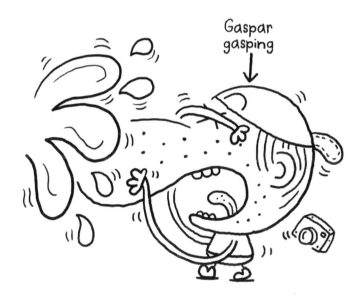

Gaspar gasping

I looked at the album, floating in the punch, and then at Nancy, a droplet of Fronkle zigzagging down her cheek like an invisible Snailypoos Two.

My hand went into my pocket to give her a spare napkin, and it gave me one of my keel ideas.

'By the power of non-smelly ski-outfit knee!' I shouted, and I lifted the dripping album from the bowl and whipped my entire napkin collection out.

panic
stations

I grabbed a handful of napkins and
started dabbing them on to Nancy's
soggy stamps, feeling like the doctor in
my mum's second-favourite TV show.

The only problem was, I'm not a
doctor.

The more I dabbed, the more the stamps started sticking on to the napkins so that in the end all there was was one great big squelchy stamp-and-napkin snowball, which hadn't been my plan, thank you very much indeed.

actually kind of keel

Nancy

me

'Looks like you two are stuck-eth together!' said Bunky, doing a massive grin, and I snortled, because now that all Nancy's stamps are stuck to my napkins, we're gonna HAVE to stay friends.

'I suppose it does,' mumbled Nancy, and she did one of her smiles and stamped her little foot on to my big toe, which really really really really really really hurt.

about to tread on this

The song that'd been playing came to
an end, and a new one started tinkling
out of the speakers.

thinks
he's the
keelest

'This is going out to all the mumsys!'
boomed DJ Anton Mildew as the
Feeko's advert tune echoed around
Darren's living room and into my
earholes.

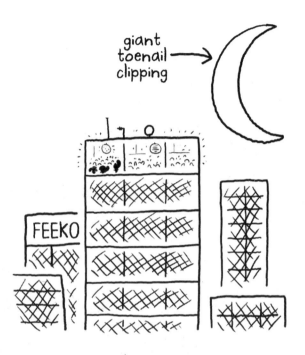

giant
toenail
clipping →

FEEKO

'Get your OWN mumsys!' I shouted as we ran on to the dance floor, and I stuck my tongue out and did a wink and wiggled my bum like the biggest loseroid in the whole wide world, thank you very much indeed, play it keel times a trillion, the end, amen.

Get your OWN ending

About the
nose drawer

Jim Smith is the keelest nose drawer in the whole wide world amen.

He graduated from art school with first class honours (the best you can get) and went on to create the branding for a sweet little chain of coffee shops.

He also designs cards and gifts under the name Waldo Pancake.

When people ask Jim why he draws such big noses, he turns round and looks at them with his massive nose, and they nod quietly.